POLLY pocket™

PollyWorld™

Written by Pamela Jane
Illustrated by MADA Design, Inc.

© 2006 Mattel, Inc. and/or Origin Products Ltd.
The POLLY POCKET trademark is owned by Origin Products Ltd.
Other trademarks and trade dress are owned by Mattel, Inc. or
Origin Products Ltd. Manufactured under license from Mattel, Inc.
First Edition.
All Rights Reserved.

Manufactured and printed in the United States of America.
ISBN-13: 978-0-696-23190-2
ISBN-10: 0-696-23190-5

We welcome your comments and suggestions.
Write to us at: Meredith Books, Children's Books,
1716 Locust St., Des Moines, IA 50309-3023.
Visit us online at: meredithbooks.com

Meredith® Books
Des Moines, Iowa

"OK, Polly. What's the big news?" asks Lea.
"You've been holding out on us!" says Crissy.
"I was sworn to secrecy!" explains Polly. "This
weekend is the grand opening of PollyWorld
and our class will be competing in contests and
games on national TV!"
"PollyWorld, here we come!" cries Lea.

On Friday afternoon, Samuel drives Polly and her pals to PollyWorld.

"Ladies, welcome to PollyWorld!" Samuel says, as the limo rolls up to the gates of the theme park.

Polly's pals gaze wide-eyed at the dazzling array of rides, shops, and cafes.

"I'm going to go meet my dad," says Polly. "He has a big surprise!"

Shani asks, "What could be bigger than this?"

"Dad, PollyWorld is monster fabuloriffic!" cries Polly, giving her dad a hug.

"I'm happy you like it," replies Mr. Pocket. "Polly, you know I want to give you everything in the world."

"Dad, you already have! What other girl has her own theme park?"

"There's one thing I haven't given you," says Mr. Pocket. "You don't have a—"

Just then, in breezes a beautiful young woman.
"You must be Polly!" she says. "I'd hug you, but I don't want to be pushy with the 'new mom' thing."

Polly looks stunned. "The new . . . what?"

"Polly," says Mr. Pocket. "Lorelai and I are getting married. I'll be able to give you the one thing you don't have—a mom."

"Gee," says Polly slowly, "that sounds—"

"Terrific, doesn't it?" interrupts Lorelai.

"What do you think about our wedding plans, Polly?" Mr. Pocket asks.

"Ah, well . . . it's an awfully big surprise," says Polly slowly.

"John, don't put her on the spot!" says Lorelai. "Let her get used to the idea of a new mom, while I get to know my super-cool new daughter!"

Back in their room, Polly tells her pals about her dad's surprise. At first, her friends are excited. Everyone talks at once.

"We can be guests at the wedding!"

Shani notices that Polly is quiet.

"What's wrong, Polly?" she asks.

"I want my dad to be happy," says Polly, "but Lorelai is acting like she's my mom."

"Maybe she just needs some time," says Crissy.

At Pollynesian Paradise, the teams compete in a Hula Duela dance.

"Surf's up!" says Lea. "Here we go!"

"One, two, three, four, five!" yells Beth. "I'm the one who will survive!"

"I have no clue how to hula!" cries Lila.

"Sock it to them, Team Pocket!" shouts Samuel. "Err—I mean, bravo."

Down Polly and Lila go, into the rolling surf.

"And the winner is . . . Team Beth!"

"Chillax, girls!" says Polly. "We'll win next time."

Beth ducks into the powder room where she overhears Lorelai talking on the phone.

"Polly is pretty, talented, and smart, and her dad adores her!" Lorelai whispers. "There's only one way I can compete with that—get John to send her away to boarding school and make him think it's his idea!"

"Brilliant!" says Beth, coming up behind Lorelai.

Startled, Lorelai turns around. "I don't know what you think you heard, but—"

"Relax!" says Beth. "I'm a friend—yours, that is. I have a plan to help."

"Do tell."

"Rule No. 1," says Beth. "Know your enemy. Hang out with Polly and her pals!"

Lorelai smiles. "I see a major shopping spree in my future."

Lorelai takes Polly and her friends shopping on PollyWalk.

"Lorelai, you are my new fashion hero!" says Lila.

Everyone chimes in. "Thanks for the new stuff, Lorelai!"

Polly tries a warmish smile, "Yeah, thanks."

"Tomorrow is the river raft race," says Lila. "I hope we win. Beth's team might be tough to beat."

Polly has a major lightbulb moment. "What does Beth love the most?"

Lila grins. "Seeing bad things happen to you."

"Exactly!" says Polly. "If we pretend to fight, Beth will be distracted, and we can sneak ahead and win!"

Lorelai comes up behind them. "That's brilliant!"

The next morning, Polly and her friends compete in a rollicking river race in the Rain Forest Realm.

"Go, Polly!" yells Mr. Pocket.

"John, stop putting so much pressure on her," says Lorelai. "She's stressed out enough!"

Mr. Pocket looks surprised. "Polly, stressed?"

Lorelai nods. "With school, sports, and jetting all over the world, who wouldn't be?"

Mr. Pocket smiles. "How sweet! You're concerned about Polly, just like a real mom!"

"Of course," says Lorelai. "I'm crazy about her. That's why I'm worried."

"Don't worry too much about Polly," says Mr. Pocket. "She's very mature for her age."

On the river, Polly and her pals pretend to get into a huge fight!

"Is this my birthday?" asks Beth. "Because I'm getting the best present in the world—Polly and her pals in a major battle!"

Mr. Pocket looks worried.

"That's strange. Polly and her friends never fight," he says. "Something must be—"

"Terribly wrong?" asks Lorelai.

Mr. Pocket nods slowly. "Maybe you're right about Polly. What did your parents do when you were her age?"

Lorelai tries to hide a smile.

"They sent me to boarding school," she says. "Of course, I put up a fight at first, but it turned out to be great."

Polly's plan works. Team Pocket wins the river race!

Back in the hotel, Polly is shocked to see Samuel walk out carrying his suitcases.

"S-Man, you're not leaving, are you?"

"I'm taking a leave of absence," says Samuel.

"But I need you here," says Polly. "Please don't go!"

"You deserve a family, Polly," says Samuel. "I'm in the way."

"Did Lorelai put you up to this?"

"Don't worry, Polly," says Samuel. "Things will work out for the best."

Back in her dad's room, Polly tells her dad about Samuel leaving, and Mr. Pocket breaks the news about boarding school.

"But I don't want to go away to school! All my friends and family are here!"

"I know you're upset, sweetheart, but I'm sure this is best," says Mr. Pocket. "I'll fly up to see you every weekend."

Polly's friends are shocked to hear the news.
"What will we do without you?"
"What about the band?"
"I won't be gone forever," says Polly. "Just for . . . awhile."
"Tonight will be the last performance of Polly and the Pockets," says Crissy sadly.
"Let's make it a night to remember!" says Shani, hugging Polly.

It is a day to remember too. Team Polly
competes in an Extreme Scavenger Hunt.

The girls stretch a giant licorice stick across
PollyWorld . . .

write their names in lights on PollyWalk . . .

and take a hair-raising ride on PollyWhirl.

"I thought you would be more upset about
going to boarding school," says Beth.

"How did you know about that?" asks Polly.

"I'm psychic!" says Beth.

Team Polly gives it their all, but Team Thrash
beats them to the finish line!

"Look at this DVD footage I shot during the
Scavenger Hunt!" says Shani, back at the room.
The girls gather around the computer.
"No way!" says Polly. "It's Lorelai and Beth!"
"Well?" Beth asks. "Did you get Polly's dad to
send her to boarding school?"
"The deed is done!" says Lorelai.
Beth gives two thumbs-up. "Yes!"

"If I show this to my dad, he'll never marry Lorelai!" says Polly.

"What are we waiting for, girls?" cries Shani. "Let's go!"

Outside they see Mr. Pocket with his arm around Lorelai.

"You're one of a kind, John," says Lorelai. "That's why I fell for you."

"I'm lucky you did," says Mr. Pocket.

"Let's get out of here!" whispers Polly.

"What's wrong?" asks Crissy, when they are safely away. "Aren't you going to show the DVD to your dad?"

"I can't," says Polly. "Did you see them together? Lorelai makes my dad happy, and he deserves that."

Polly breaks the DVD into pieces.

"Bye-bye, evidence," says Shani.

"Come on," says Polly. "Let's go practice our new song!"

Polly and her friends set up their band at the arena. Just as they begin, a trapdoor on stage flies open, sending them all tumbling down into the dark.

The girls land in a heap beneath the stage.

"Help!" yells Lila.

"No one can hear us!" says Polly. "We're trapped!"

Polly's Rockin' Arena is filling up. TV cameras begin to roll.

"This is the final competition!" announces the TV host. "Our first competitor is Team Thrash!" The boys begin a routine on skates, skateboards, and bikes.

Behind the curtain, Beth pulls a rope and dozens of balls bounce out on stage. The team members barely keep their balance.

"Hear that?" asks Beth. The audience is laughing at them. "We are so winning this thing!"

Next, the TV host announces Polly and the
Pockets. There is huge applause, but no sign of
the band.

Mr. Pocket looks worried. "Something must
be wrong. Polly never misses a performance!"

Under the stage, Polly and her friends
stumble around in the dark.

"Ouch!" cries Crissy. "I banged my ankle
on something!"

"A lever!" says Polly. "This could be our
way out!"

They all pull together. Slowly the floor begins to rise. A moment later Polly and the Pockets are on stage, magically dressed to rock and ready to roll!

The audience goes wild.

"Thank goodness, nothing went wrong!" says Mr. Pocket.

"Except my plans!" mutters Beth. "Polly and the Pockets will win big-time tonight, unless I can shut down the sound!"

Beth leans over and whispers to Lorelai.
"Come with me to the control booth!"
    "Can't you see I'm busy?" snaps Lorelai.
    "This is urgent!" says Beth.
    Lorelai and Beth sneak off to the control booth.
    "I need you to help me cut the sound so Polly
and the Pockets won't win tonight," says Beth.

"Why should I help you?" asks Lorelai. "I have everything I want."

"Because if you don't, I'll tell Mr. Pocket all your secrets!"

Beth leans back, accidentally hitting a button that projects her and Lorelai onto a huge TV screen above the arena. Beth's moment of fame has arrived—only she doesn't know it!

"I'll tell Polly's dad how you were jealous of Polly and schemed to send her off to boarding school," says Beth, her voice echoing through the arena.

"Go ahead," says Lorelai. "He won't believe you. I have John Pocket wrapped around my finger!"

The audience gasps, and Lorelai whirls around. She and Beth are on TV, with the entire world watching and listening!

"Cut the switch!" shouts Lorelai. But it is too late. Mr. Pocket bursts into the booth.

"Our engagement is off, Lorelai," he says. "And Polly will NOT be going to boarding school."

"But . . . but," stutters Lorelai.

"I'm on TV!" cries Beth. "Welcome to BethWorld!" She leaps into the air and crashes to the floor with a loud thump. The audience roars.

In the end, Team Thrash wins the competition for its extreme clown routine.

"Just wait until next time," mumbles Beth, as the arena rocks out to the music of Polly and the Pockets on the best weekend ever in PollyWorld.